SAM HAIN
OCCULT DETECTIVE

A NIGHT IN
KNIGHTSBRIDGE

E

GW00481982

~

www.bronjames.co.uk
www.samhainscasebook.co.uk

SAM HAIN
A NIGHT IN KNIGHTSBRIDGE

PROLOGUE

At the end of a long and stressful day, Elena Turner stepped into the shower. Her time had been spent, rather tediously, sorting out the study; unpacking boxes, moving furniture, and setting up the computer. A lot of the stuff had already been unboxed and simply needed organising. She'd moved one of the bookcases to put it by the side of the desk, only to discover that rising damp had started growing up the wall and on the back of the bookcase, even spreading to damage a number of the as-yet-unpacked boxes too. Moving house was rarely a relaxing experience at the best of times, without the furniture getting covered in mould too.

Between cleaning mould off of the walls and shelves and anything else that had been damaged, Elena also had to look after Charlie, her seven-year-old son. By the time she'd finished cleaning everything and had moved the bookcases back to where they should be, and Charlie was happily playing with his dinosaur toys in the living room, everything looked exactly the way it had done before she had even started that morning. Her husband, Lloyd, had not been happy when he came home only to find that nothing had been done in *his* study (despite the fact that they'd agreed it was a shared work room). Quite why he couldn't do it himself, especially if it really was as easy as he kept saying it was, was beyond her.

Another wasted day, she thought to herself, turning the shower taps as far as they would go. A powerful stream of steaming hot water shot out of the shower-head. Closing her eyes, she tipped her head back and let the water spray onto her face and trickle down her body. She was quite ready to call it a day, just relax in the shower for quarter of an hour and then get into bed. Not that she was getting much sleep at the moment, anyway. She rolled her head around, feeling the aching tension that had been built up in her shoulders, and sighed.

She'd only been in the shower five minutes when she suddenly heard something crashing. Opening her eyes, she paused and listened out for anything else, but heard nothing. Turning off the shower, she stepped out into the steam-filled bathroom, wrapping a towel around herself. Over in the corner she could see that the contents of the cabinet had emptied out onto the floor, the cabinet's door hanging wide open. Shampoo and conditioner bottles were strewn about the room, and numerous other cosmetics lay in a pile beneath the cabinet. Elena picked up the scattered toiletries and started to put them carefully back in the cabinet. She closed the cabinet's door, and stepped back in fear. Across the steamed-up surface of the cabinet's mirrored door, in big, capital letters, were these words.

THE VOID AWAKENS. DARKNESS IS COMING.

'Very funny!' Elena said sarcastically, walking into the living room with her dressing gown wrapped around her, her hair hidden up inside the large beehive-like towel on her head. Lloyd was sat in the armchair by the fireplace, reading a book.

'What've I done now?'

'The writing in the mirror. You know how spooked I've been about all this ghost stuff recently. I don't like you taking the piss out of me like this!'

Ever since moving in, Elena had been convinced she'd seen a ghost wandering around the house, and on occasion had thought she'd seen it knocking crockery off of the kitchen counters. Sometimes she even thought she could hear someone whispering to her in the dead of night (although she couldn't hear what they were saying), or walking up the stairs and opening and closing doors. There was never anybody there, though.

'What writing in the mirror?' Lloyd had a look of genuine confusion on his face. Elena felt her heart sink. If it had been him, he would have had that irritating smirk plastered across his face.

'That wasn't you?'

'I haven't done anything. Wasn't Charlie?'

'Darling, I don't mean to sound sarky, but do

you really think a seven-year-old would write a message of foreboding like "the void awakens, darkness is coming," on a mirror he can't even reach?'

Lloyd sat in a vacant silence. He briefly glanced down at his book, and then back up to Elena. He cleared his throat uncomfortably. 'No, I suppose not.'

Fiddling nervously with one of the rings on her fingers, Elena sat down in the chair opposite her husband. She gazed distantly into the fireplace, lost in thought. 'We need a psychic, a medium or an exorcist or something,' she said conclusively. Lloyd looked up at her sceptically, and returned to reading his book.

CHAPTER I

It had been a slow week for Sam Hain.

The life of an occult detective was a strange and unpredictable one, one which was often spent dealing with the weird and the fantastical, but, much like most other walks of life, the supernatural sleuth would hit the occasional slump. There was the odd mysterious occurrence, inexplicable bursts of light in the sky or things that went bump in the night, but Sam was starting to feel bored. The transmundane was beginning to seem more and more mundane. The most interesting case that had been presented to him that week, which had promised to be an exciting hunt for a particularly destructive poltergeist, turned out to be little more than a mischievous and clumsy cat.

It was only while he was browsing the internet one evening, perusing paranormal forums for a good mystery or extraordinary event to sink his teeth into, that Sam finally found something that sparked his interest. It was exactly the kind of thing he'd been looking for and, he thought, a good introductory case for his new associate, Alice Carroll.

It had been over a month since Alice had last seen Sam. Their first and last meeting – when Alice had been haunted by the visions of a being from another realm on Halloween – had left her feeling like she'd tumbled down the rabbit hole into a world far stranger than she could ever have imagined. She had checked out the occult detective's website shortly after their first encounter, to try to find out more about this strange man. His blog hadn't really given her much more of an insight into the life of Sam Hain; he didn't update it very regularly, and when he did it was either to write brief overviews of former cases or vague, mysterious posts.

Since then, Alice had been feeding her curiosity, trying to learn more about the supernatural world and researching the paranormal (when she wasn't busy with work), and she'd tried to keep in touch with Sam as and when she could. He wasn't the easiest person to keep in contact with, and at one point she didn't hear from him for over a week, but he always got back to her in the end.

She'd been asking him about his line of work, enquiring about the supernatural and learning more about the wondrous and fantastical things which exist just outside of the boundaries of reality. In between being cryptically vague about his own experiences, Sam had suggested a number of resources for Alice to read through, but warned her that in amongst the mystery, intrigue and magick, darker forces often lurk in the shadows.

As much as Alice's own experience had left her feeling shaken, and Sam's sinister and foreboding warnings had further added to her fear, she felt far too intrigued to simply turn away from all of this now. A part of her still remained dubious, but her own curiosity drove her to find out more.

In her spare time, she'd browsed the websites Sam had recommended, with a mix of fascination and cynicism. Some of the "eye-witness" testimonies and rumoured happenings sounded like works of fiction, and others were clearly written by people who were desperate to find something extraordinary in the ordinary (her favourite of these was the idea that all clouds were secretly alien spaceships, simply disguised as clouds so they didn't startle anyone), but amongst them all there were a few cases which Alice thought seemed credible. Some even bore similarities to her own experiences.

In addition, Sam had also sent her what he called his official manual, or as she'd now dubbed it: Demonology for Dummies. It wasn't so much a manual as it was a large, well-worn notebook with Sam's handwriting scrawled across its pages in an almost entirely illegible manner. Amongst the pages of scribbled sentences and bullet-pointed notes from former cases were a handful of poorly drawn illustrations of things Alice couldn't even begin to recognise. Somewhere towards the middle of the book, between a page about metaphysical parasites and something about interdimensional portals, was a surprisingly normal shopping list.

Alice had only briefly skimmed over the pages of the notebook, but amongst the scrawlings and indecipherable text, some of it had caught her interest. Before meeting Sam, she had never really given the supernatural much thought – not since childhood, anyway – and had it not been for him then she probably would have ended up seeing a therapist about her delusions. But everything Sam had introduced her to since Halloween had reignited her imagination and opened her eyes to a new world. She wanted to discover and experience these things first hand and, after much deliberation, she decided to take Sam up on his offer. She was ready to join him on one of his cases.

One evening, after amusing herself with reading the latest blog post on a website titled "Clouds: What are they really?", she sent Sam a message asking about joining him on one of his adventures, and waited. It was almost three days before he replied to her, and when he did it was ambiguous and brief.

Would be my pleasure, the message read, *have just the thing in mind. Meet in Knightsbridge, outside the tube station, tonight, 6pm. -SH*

The evening was cold and windy, as many a winter night tended to be in London. The stars were blotted out by a sickeningly beige mass of clouds hanging low over the city, and the occasional cold spattering of rain added an extra chill to the air. Christmas decorations adorned every shop and street, and the roads of

Knightsbridge were alive with shoppers, rushing about in the bright lights of the street and the warm glow of the shop windows.

Standing outside of the London Underground station, Alice pulled her coat tightly around herself and folded her arms. She'd been waiting in the cold for a quarter of an hour now, and was staring longingly at the people who were settling down to large mugs of coffee in warm, cosy-looking cafés. Sam had only told her to meet him there at that time, nothing of what they were going to be doing and, despite her intrigue, Alice was starting to feel nervous. She habitually checked the time on her phone. Sam was now ten minutes late. Glancing around, she noticed a familiar silhouette striding towards her, overcoat billowing out behind it and hat slightly slanting to the right.

Sam Hain walked up to her, and tipped the rim of his hat in greeting.

'You're late!' Alice mockingly accosted him.

'I'm never late! I may not always be on time, but I turn up exactly when I'm meant to,' he retorted, a wry grin on his face. 'Hope you weren't waiting too long.'

'Only twenty minutes or so. Could do with warming up a bit.' She looked longingly at one of the inviting cafés. It looked warm and comfortable in there; its rosy-cheeked customers reclined luxuriously on cushiony sofas, their winter coats draped over the backs of their seats, as they sipped from large mugs piled high with whipped cream and marshmallows, with decadent slices of cake on the tables next to them. Decorated fir trees glittered festively, standing several feet taller than the customers, filling the place with Christmas cheer.

'Let's find somewhere to go and warm up then,' Sam said, and he started to head down the road towards the parade of shops.

The chip shop they soon found themselves in was fairly standard as far as chip shops were concerned. The white tiled floor was by no means shiny, slightly grimy from the occasional dropped and trampled food and splatterings of vinegar and ketchup, but still the floor glared under the fluorescent lights. As they entered, Sam and Alice were greeted by the sight of the Happy Fish (for that is what the shop was called), a large cartoonish cod standing proudly by the counter, a broad smile across its face and giving a reassuring thumbs up in the direction of the door. This was not nearly as reassuring as it was probably meant to be, because – as Sam rightly pointed out – fish do not have thumbs with which to give a thumbs up, nor are they able to smile broadly. Secondly, the overly cheery mascot was completely at odds with the man behind the counter, who glared at nothing in particular while he miserably shovelled chips into small polystyrene boxes.

The man grunted as he thrust two polystyrene boxes over the counter, and scattered the change for the chips vaguely in Sam's direction. Holding the boxes in one hand and scooping up his change, as well as some unidentifiable crumbs, with the other, Sam walked over to the table where Alice was sitting. He placed one of the portions in front of her, taking a seat in the uncomfortable plastic chair opposite her. Producing two tiny chip-forks from his coat pocket, he handed one to her. She looked at him and raised a sarcastic eyebrow.

'You really know how to treat a lady...'

'Well, I'm sorry I couldn't see any empty seats in the other cafés! Anyway, it's sort of all right here, isn't it?'

The man who had gruntingly served them came to the table carrying their two cups of coffee. He indelicately placed the polystyrene cups down on the table, spilling coffee on Sam's chips in the process, grunted again, and walked away. Sam looked dejectedly at his now coffee-soaked chips, and picked one up to inspect it. The chip flopped loosely between his fingers, dripping with murky brown coffee. With a tentative nibble, he gave a surprised 'hmm!' and a strangely approving nod. Alice sampled one of her chips (without a coffee dressing), and discovered that it was actually quite good. The coffee, she learned, was disappointing at best.

'So, how've you been?' Sam eventually asked, through a mouthful of chips.

'Fine, I suppose. No demons have tried to set up camp in my head, so all things considered I'd say I'm doing pretty well,' Alice said. She treated the situation with more levity now than she had at the time, but the memory of what happened that night still made her feel uneasy.

'Always a good thing,' he nodded, taking a gulp of his coffee and grimacing.

'And how have things been with you? Any exciting adventures?' She asked.

'Bored, mostly. Things have been quite quiet, no paranormal phenomena really worth investigating,' he paused momentarily, as he thought about everything he'd done since they'd last met. 'Most of my cases recently have turned out to be nothing more than faulty plumbing, clumsy cats and some easily spooked clients. Actually, you were my last interesting case,' he added. It sounded almost as if Sam had complimented Alice, but it was difficult to tell.

'So, I'm curious... What are we doing here?' She looked at Sam and noticed a glint in his eyes. 'And before you say anything, I know we're eating chips.' The glint disappeared, and he looked down at his chips, disappointed, as if she'd just spoiled the punchline.

'Well,' he began, and leaned in, taking care to not plant his elbow in any of the spilt coffee, 'you recall that around the time I met you, there was something about "darkness is coming"?'

Alice nodded and a cold frisson ran down her spine. She shivered involuntarily as she recalled the demon's ominous words.

'I've been doing some searching,' Sam continued, 'trying to find any other references to it. I've seen signs, heard whispers, but nothing substantial. For a while, it seemed like yours was an isolated case, the only direct incident, but then

I found this...' He trailed off as he reached into his coat pocket and pulled out a small notebook. He removed some poorly folded sheets of paper from between its pages and pushed them across the table to her. Intrigued, Alice unfolded the pages and examined them.

'There's a house just around the corner that's apparently being haunted by a poltergeist,' he said, as Alice looked over the information he'd printed out.

On the first page in a large, bold typeface was the title: "Help! I think my house is haunted." It was a post on a forum for would-be ghost hunters, written by a woman named Elena Turner. She had recently moved into a new house in the Knightsbridge area with her husband and seven-year-old son, and after just one viewing they had put an offer in immediately. The estate agent had been delighted to sell the property so soon. Although the Turners had fallen in love with their new home almost immediately, ever since moving in Elena had felt a lingering sense of uneasiness. She initially put this down to the stress and panic everyone suffered when moving house, and she didn't think much of it at first and simply carried on as usual. That was until last week, when things had taken a turn for the inexplicable.

The next page showed photographs, taken on Elena's phone, of broken crockery and smashed glass tumblers – allegedly targeted by the ghost – and a picture of the staircase in which "the shadow of a person can clearly be seen." It was more of a vaguely humanoid-shaped patch in the image that was a slightly darker shade than the rest of it, and Alice was starting to feel sceptical. It wasn't until she turned to the next page that something caught her attention.

'Darkness is coming,' Sam said as Alice read the words. Another photograph showed the three words written on the steamed-up surface of a bathroom mirror, along with the equally ominous "the void awakens." Although this kind of evidence for ghostly activity could easily be faked, the fact that it echoed Alice's own experience with the supernatural couldn't be ignored.

'This can't be coincidence,' Alice said, and Sam nodded in agreement.

'No such thing as a coincidence. The Universe is rarely so lazy.'

The post continued to describe how things would move seemingly without cause, and sometimes things would mysteriously disappear. Nothing quite as simple as a pair of glasses or a set of keys, these things had a habit of vanishing by themselves, but at one point the butter dish went missing from the fridge for an hour, before reappearing again on one of the arm chairs in the living room with less butter than it had left with. On other occasions, cups and plates would smash, as if they were pushed off of the kitchen counters by an invisible hand. Disembodied noises could be heard throughout the house, like someone moving furniture or knocking on the door, and Elena sometimes thought she could hear someone whispering to her. Her son also suffered from recurring nightmares of being chased by monsters, which Elena was now sure was connected to the haunting.

'I got in touch with the woman who wrote this earlier this week, and I've offered to investigate their situation. She and her husband are expecting me there this evening. I was wondering, if you're interested, whether you'd like to join me on the case?' Sam grinned at Alice. He already knew her answer.

'Absolutely!' She exclaimed, and the man behind the counter looked up and grunted in admonishment. With a final gulp of the drink that wasn't quite coffee, Sam stood up and threw his coat on.

'Let's get going, then.'

CHAPTER II

The night was even colder than before, and a light fog was starting to settle on the city. Alice and Sam walked along the darkened road towards a terrace of tall and slender Victorian houses which overlooked a small private garden in the middle of Cadmus Square. As they approached the Turners' home, Sam strode purposefully up the path towards the front door and knocked. A light came on in the hallway, dimly lighting the doorstep from a small window above the door frame. From behind the door, they could hear the sound of jangling keys, the repeated clunking of the lock, and a man angrily muttering 'bloody thing...' Eventually, the door swung open to reveal a ginger-haired man in a comfortable-looking green jumper, a haggard look on his face.

'Good evening. I'm Sam Hain – occult detective and expert in all things supernatural – and this is my friend and colleague Alice Carroll. We're here about your ghost.' Sam stood proudly and straightened his coat lapels with an air of self-importance.

'Ah, yes, Elena said we'd be expecting you. Lloyd, Lloyd Turner,' the man replied, and turned to head back inside. 'Come in, then,' he said, gesturing for them to follow him, 'you'll have to excuse the mess, we only moved in last month.'

The house was not in a mess. For a house that had only been moved into a month previously, it was astoundingly neat. There were no traces of boxes or of furniture that had yet to find its place in the home, and the house itself was spotless. Lloyd led Sam and Alice through to the living room, where the lights were on low and an open fireplace burned and crackled contently, bathing the room in a warm glow.

'Take a seat, I'll be back in a moment,' Lloyd said, indicating an arrangement of green velvet armchairs by the fireside. Alice and Sam sat down as their host left the room, and the head of Elena Turner peered around the door.

'I'll be with you in a sec, just making some tea,' she said, and her head disappeared back behind the door again.

Sam peered around the room with curiosity. The four armchairs were seated a comfortable distance from the fire, which seemed to be the heart of the room. A spotless coffee table sat in the middle of the armchairs. Two bookcases stood in the corner by the front window, their shelves lined with a vast array of books from the complete collection of Shakespeare's plays to the numerous works by Plato. Various ornaments and pictures decorated the rest of the room. The place was incredibly well-kept, which, for a house that had only recently been moved into and was allegedly being terrorised by a ghost, was nothing short of incredible. Sam had stood up to look at the picture hanging above the fireplace (a piece reminiscent of van Gogh) when Elena and Lloyd returned, carrying in a tray of tea and a small selection of biscuits. Elena placed the tray down on the coffee table. Sam sat back down, and poured himself a cup.

Lloyd reclined in the seat opposite the two of them. His ginger hair and beard seemed to be ablaze in the fire-light, and his eyes were a very prominent shade of green. He took a sip of his tea, and placed it back on its saucer. His wife sat down next to him. Elena Turner was a mousey-haired woman, and she appeared to be several years younger than her husband, but signs of ageing were beginning to show around her brown eyes. Both of them looked like they had not had a decent night's sleep in several weeks.

'So, Mister Hain. Your message said you might be able to help with our, uhm, problem,' Elena said.

'Indeed, I believe I can,' Sam said, and he leaned forward towards the pair of them. 'I'll need your utmost trust in this matter, though. Both of you.'

Elena nodded. 'Of course.'

Lloyd simply replied with a sceptical 'hrrmm.'

'Excellent!' Sam clapped his hands together, and leaned back into the armchair. 'Well then, could you please describe exactly what's been going on here.'

'Well, we moved in about a month ago, and

everything was fine,' Elena started to explain. 'We began unpacking, getting the house together and decorating, and that's when the trouble started. I wrote about most of it on the forum. You know, things like cups breaking, as if someone was pushing them off of the sides, and strange noises in the night. I've even seen these, uh, apparitions. Of a person, like a ghost, upstairs on the landing.'

Sam nodded as he listened to Elena's account, although he already knew most of the details. Lloyd hadn't said a word about any of it and had simply sat there, sipping his tea and watching Sam with a sceptical eye from over the rim of his teacup.

'And what about you, Mister Turner?' Sam enquired. 'Have you experienced any of this supernatural activity?'

Lloyd Turner was a stoic looking man; he was the kind of person who could break his leg, wince for a second, and almost instantly return to stone-faced neutrality as if nothing had happened. His face remained unchanging as he answered.

'I'm not going to lie to you, Mister Hain. I'm not a believer in ghosts. There are often perfectly reasonable, rational explanations to what others may attribute to the supernatural.'

'And what of the writing in the bathroom mirror?' Sam asked, removing the crumpled paper from his pocket and pointing at the picture of the steamed-up mirror. 'When did this happen?'

'This was taken about a week ago,' Elena said, taking the paper from Sam and looking at the image. 'We can't think of any explanation for it. What do you make of it, Mister Hain?'

'Please, call me Sam. And that's what I'm here to find out,' he said, consulting one of the other pieces of paper he'd printed off. 'You also mentioned your son has been having recurring nightmares?'

Elena nodded. 'Yes, ever since we moved here Charlie's had dreams that he's being chased by monsters. He often wakes up in tears...'

'Okay. Well, I already have my suspicions about what we're dealing with here. Would it be all right with you both if my colleague and I stayed a while to figure things out?'

'Of course,' Elena said with a faint smile.

'Thank you.' Sam stood up and made his way towards the living room door. 'Just one more thing, Misses Turner-'

'Just call me Elena.'

'Okay then. Just one more thing, Elena, do you know if you have any electrical issues in this house?'

'Not that I'm aware of, why do you ask?' Elena answered.

'Fuses can be a bit of a bugger sometimes,' Lloyd contributed.

'Oh, it's just that your lights appear to be flickering.'

The lights were indeed flickering, and despite the fireplace lighting up most of the room, the fluctuating brightening and dimming of the lightbulbs was slowly becoming more and more noticeable.

'I don't know if you've noticed this before, but in cases like this, paranormal activity is often preceded by disruptions to electrics,' Sam said, and as if on cue the lights went out completely, leaving the room lit only by the warm light of the fire.

'See. This is exactly the kind of thing I mean,' Elena said.

'Damn fuse has blown again...' Lloyd said as he stood up and made his way out of the room to find the fusebox.

Alice walked over and stood by Sam's side, looking around the room nervously. 'What's going on?'

He brashly shushed her and stood silently, surveying the room, searching for the faintest hint of activity. Nothing happened. He turned to Elena. 'Does this happen a lot?'

'It's happened four times now, two in the past week alone,' she replied, looking nervously around the darkened room.

Alice moved slowly into the centre of the room. She felt something unusual, something almost like the prelude to a thunderstorm but with decidedly less rain. The air had become stale, unmoving, and the atmosphere in the room became inexplicably heavy. It was as if the pressure in the room was slowly building up. There was a sudden, loud bang as something hit the floor, causing Alice and Elena to jump. It startled Sam, too, but he tried not to show it.

A book had fallen off of one of the shelves, landing at the foot of the bookcase, as if someone had simply pushed it off. There was no slant in the shelves or the room to suggest it was simply an act of gravity. Tentatively making his way over to it, Sam bent down to examine the book.

'Hmm, Edgar Allan Poe,' he said with a tone of approval, and was struck in the back of the head by another book. 'Christ almighty...' He muttered, rubbing where it had hit.

Another book flew off of the shelf, striking Sam again, and another propelled itself towards Alice. She ducked just in time, narrowly dodging *War and Peace*, and it struck the wall behind her with a papery thud. *A Remembrance of Things Past* flew over Sam's head and soared straight into the door. Elena had scurried over to take cover behind the door, holding it open and using it like a shield, and Sam and Alice quickly followed her example. They strategically retreated to the door, ducking and weaving as the bookcase continued to take pot-shots at them, and finally took shelter just outside of the bookcase's firing arc.

The minute all three of them were behind the door, books stopped flying off of the shelves and the lights suddenly flickered back into life. Alice felt the pressure in the room lift and return to normal, as if someone had just opened a window and a gust of fresh air had blown through the place. Sam moved back into the middle of the room, and looked around. Several books now lay strewn across the room, but there were no other signs of disturbance. Elena began to pick up the books and return them to their shelves, and Alice started to help her while Sam stood obliviously looking around the room.

'Had to turn the bloody fusebox off and on again,' Lloyd announced, returning to the now perfectly lit room. It took him a few moments to notice that things weren't quite how he'd left them. 'Why're my books on the floor?'

'Had a bit of an incident. Your ghost started throwing things at us,' Sam said. 'If it's all right with you, we'll stay to investigate this room a bit further.'

Elena nodded in agreement. 'Will you need us to stay in here too?'

'No, no,' Sam replied, 'just go about your evening as usual and we'll see what happens. I'll let you know as soon as I have something.'

'Thank you,' Elena said, and Lloyd nodded in resigning agreement, 'we'll leave you to it then.' The two of them left the room to go about their evening, leaving Sam and Alice to get to work. As the sound of footsteps slowly making their way up the stairs grew fainter and fainter, Alice was sure she could hear Lloyd's voice grumbling 'bloody ghost nonsense.'

When the Turners were finally upstairs, Sam took the last sip of tea from his cup, and walked over to the offending bookcase. Reaching into the breast pocket of his jacket, he withdrew a strange, rod-like device. It was a short metallic thing, gleaming and chrome-like, probably no more than ten inches long and about an inch in diameter. At its tip was a pointed quartz crystal, and at the opposite end a polished black stone. Alice thought it resembled a sort of technological wand, as if PC World had opened a new department for the modern mage.

Sam started to move the device slowly around the outside of the bookcase, waving it along the shelves. The crystal at the wand's tip seemed to glow with a soft light, brightening and dimming at intervals, and Alice thought she could hear a faint humming sound coming from it. Every now and again, Sam would nod and 'hmm' knowledgeably, briefly examining the device or giving it a tap, and carried on with waving it around.

'What are you doing?' Alice asked, somewhat perplexed as Sam continued to waft the thing about like some kind of interpretative dance.

'I'm checking the energy disturbance around the bookcase,' Sam said, and with a final flourishing wave of the device, he put it back in his coat pocket. 'There's still some residual energy traces from when whatever it was was throwing books at us.'

He knelt down next to the bookcase and, producing a small piece of chalk from his back pocket, he quickly drew a five-pointed star, muttering something which sounded like an incantation under his breath.

'What are you doing now?' Alice asked, looking over to the occult detective, knelt on the floor quite happily defacing a stranger's carpet. 'Stop drawing Satanic symbols on the Turners' carpet!'

'It's not Satanic,' he said wearily, 'it's a pentagram, a symbol of magickal protection. Its five points represent the four elements: Earth, Air, Fire and Water. Plus the fifth element: Magick, Arcana, Spirit, call it what you will. It represents the binding and controlling of the elements in magick, to protect the user. It'll keep us safe from more incidents, in this room at least.' He drew a circle around the star, encasing the pentagram, and he turned to face Alice. He saw her dubious expression. 'Don't worry, the chalk will lift right out with a good hoover.'

'So what do you think it was then? A ghost?'

'Almost certainly,' Sam said. He fell back into one of the chairs, bouncing slightly as he landed. 'It's not just a passive apparition either, it's interacting with the physical world and threatening that darkness is coming...' He held his chin between his forefinger and thumb, running them back and forth over his stubble as he thought.

'Just before all of that happened, I felt something. Like pressure was increasing. It was like the room was building up to what was about to happen,' Alice said, hoping Sam might be able to shed some light on what she'd sensed.

'That would've been the increase of localised energy in the Akashic Field. It takes a fair amount of effort for something incorporeal to interact with things on our plane of existence.'

'The whatty field?' Alice looked confused.

'*Akashic* Field. Didn't you read the manual?' He

sounded almost accusatory.

'Some of it!' She retorted. 'Just, y'know, not actually the part you're talking about.'

'The Akashic Field is a zero-point subspace nexus that permeates the entirety of existence,' Sam said plainly, as if he was explaining that water is wet. Alice simply stared at him vacantly.

'Could you talk like a normal human being for a change, please?'

'It's kind of like an underlying energy field that connects everything in the Universe. Everything's interconnected, everything bound by the Field to some extent. With the right knowledge, one can feel the Field, learn to tap into its energies, and even come to use it to interact with the world around them.'

Alice nodded with a vague sense of understanding. 'Like the Force in *Star Wars*?'

'Like the Force in *Star Wars*,' Sam said with a smile.

'So the ghost was Obi-Wan Kenobi-ing those books at us?'

'In a sense... Because the Akashic Field links me to, say, that book there, with the right mental discipline and concentration, I could pick it up and flick to a particular page, read it, and put it back on the shelf, all without lifting a finger.'

'And can you?' Alice asked eagerly.

'No,' he said flatly. He wished he could. 'Anyway, whenever something or someone uses the Akashic Field to interact with the physical world, it causes a temporary increase in the amount of Akasha energy in the area.'

'And that's the weird feeling I had just before things started flying off the shelves? The build-up of Akasha energy?'

Sam nodded. 'Yes.'

'How do you know all this stuff?' Alice asked. What sounded like nonsense to most people was absolute perfect sense to Sam. The reverse was probably also true.

Sam simply waved dismissively at her. 'I had a Guide,' he said, standing up and starting to pace around the room. He wandered back and forth, occasionally stopping and looking around before carrying on. His face was a mixture of unbreakable focus and yet complete confusion, like a performance artist who'd forgotten their next act. He suddenly whirled around and pointed at Alice.

'I tell you what,' he started, and Alice suddenly had a sinking sensation, knowing what he was about to say next, 'you give it a go.'

She sighed, resigning herself to her new duty as room-pacer, and stood up. 'Okay, what am I doing?'

'Just walk around the room,' Sam said. That was somewhat apparent. 'Tell me where you feel the energy change. We're looking for particular spots in the Akashic Field where the flow of energy shifts, like little energetic eddies in the room.'

'Right, looking for energetic Eddie... And how do I know when I've found him, exactly?'

'No, *eddies*, sort of like whirlpools. Just in this case, it's not a whirlpool in water, but in a living room. You'll know when you've found one,' he said unhelpfully, throwing himself back into the armchair with a grin, watching Alice intently. She marched from one side of the room to the other and back again, and shrugged.

'Nope, I'm not getting anything,' she said.

'You're doing it too fast, not paying attention. Try to move more slowly and follow your intuition. Close your eyes if that helps,' he said. He suddenly almost sounded like a mentor.

Alice began to move around the room again, not as fast this time, and she shut her eyes. She seemed to slowly glide, as if she was being carried by the flow of an invisible current. She hovered over a spot for a second, and Sam noticed a hesitation in her step.

'Trust yourself,' he prompted her, and she found his words to be reassuring. Alice continued to hover over the spot for a second or two more before she opened her eyes and pointed at the floor.

'Okay then, here,' she announced, and there was a glimmer of triumph in her eyes.

Sam stood up and made his way over to where Alice was stood, and removed the chalk from his pocket. 'Here?' He asked as he knelt down by the spot she was pointing to.

'Yes,' Alice said.

'You sure?' He asked, teasingly.

'Relatively sure,' she nodded.

'Certain?'

'Just do whatever the hell it is you have to do, will you!'

Sam chuckled to himself as he drew a small twisting symbol on the floor. He then scurried over to another part of the room and drew another one. Putting the chalk back in his pocket, Sam dusted off his hands and headed over to the pentagram. He stood in the centre of the symbol, facing in towards the room, and pulled out a dried white leaf and a lighter from one of his pockets.

'Salvia apiana, sacred sage,' he said, holding the leaf up, 'it'll help cleanse the room, and bring the energy back to a more neutral state.' He lit the sacred sage, almost burning his fingers in the process, and a plume of thick white smoke rose from the burning leaf. It smelt herbal and musty, yet oddly refreshing. Still holding the slowly burning leaf, Sam stretched his arms out and waggled his fingers in front of him, closing his eyes.

'I invoke the elements of Earth and Water, of Air and Fire. I call upon the Spirit of the All to protect this space. May the Divine Light drive back the Darkness.' Sam then clasped his hands together in a single clap, scattering ash and what remained of the charred leaf. Bowing his head, he opened his eyes, and stepped out of the pentagram as if he was stepping over a rope with the sign "please do not walk on the grass."

'There,' he said with a sense of finality, 'that

should stop any unwanted guests from entering this room. Now then...' He rifled through the printed pages from Elena's blog. 'I think it's about time we have a look around the rest of the house.'

CHAPTER III

Standing in the hallway at the foot of the staircase, Sam and Alice looked up to the floor above. The landing was dark, but faintly illuminated by a few beams of light which escaped through an open doorway somewhere upstairs. The elongated shadow of Lloyd Turner swept across the landing as he carried a box from one room to another, muttering irritably.

'All right, I think it's best if we split up. I'll take upstairs, you take the downstairs,' Sam said.

'Wait, what? Why?' Alice asked. *I've had books thrown at me from across the room by whatever's in this house*, she thought, *you're not bloody leaving me now!*

'We'll cover more ground; the sooner we finish here, the sooner the Turners can get back to their lives.' He saw her look of concern. 'Don't worry, you'll be fine. Listen, take this,' he said, and produced a small silver pentacle pendant from his pocket, 'it'll keep you safe.'

'Won't you need it for... something?'

'No, no, don't worry about me. I've got this.' He brandished his wand-like device with a knowing smile. He spun on his heels and began to head up the stairs.

'Wait! What am I looking for?' Alice asked after him as he bounded up the stairs, two steps at a time. She wanted to make a good impression on him, but to say that she felt like a fish out of water would have been an understatement.

'Just keep a third-eye out for anything unusual,' he replied before disappearing around the corner and into the dark of the landing above.

Yeah, fine, really useful, Alice thought as she watched him leap away. *No idea what I'm even looking for... Why did I think this was a good idea?* She glanced at the pentacle pendant, its silver chain resting gently across her hand. She unfastened the catch on the chain, and hung the pentacle around her neck.

Pushing open one of the doors which led off from the hallway, Alice peered into the pitch black room beyond. She couldn't see much, only vague shapes illuminated by the small amount of light which was now coming into the room from the hallway. Fumbling around on the inside wall, she felt for the light switch and pressed down when she found it. There was a sudden twanging sound from above. The lights immediately flickered on with a dazzling white light, and Alice found herself in the Turners' kitchen.

The kitchen was a reasonably small room. The walls were lined with cabinets and counters, and a small breakfast bar jutted out into the middle of the room. By the side of the sink, Alice noticed a small pile of cups and saucers, either chipped or smashed into several pieces. She took a closer look, and recognised some of them from Elena's message. She picked up a fragment of a china teacup, and examined it. *I'm guessing these fell victim to the ghost...*

She considered what Sam had said about keeping a "third-eye out" for things, and she tried to focus on what her intuition was telling her. She'd never really paid much attention to her intuition, especially not in the way Sam was expecting her to. She often got what she called "vibes," but whenever she did get a vibe it was mostly as an abstract feeling, an indefinable sensation which more often than not made very little sense, and the more she'd try to work it out the less sense it would make. Nevertheless, she felt vaguely confident; Sam would've told her if she was wrong with what she'd felt in the living room. She just had to trust that she was right.

She tried to feel whether there was another presence in the room with her.

Nothing.

It was only when she turned to leave the kitchen that Alice suddenly felt a strange sensation run over her. There was the subtle sound of gentle movement from somewhere behind her, and she got the distinct impression that she was being watched by something. Or someone. The hairs on the back of her neck pricked up. She slowly turned to look behind her, tentatively peering out of the corner of her eye in the direction of the noise. There was nothing there.

Something quickly brushed past her leg, and she jumped backwards with a stifled shriek. Her mind raced and her heart pounded, but in a fraction of a second she saw what it was. A black, fluffy cat sat at her feet, gazing up at her. She breathed a sigh of relief, kneeling down to stroke it and feeling more than a little bit silly.

'I've never been so pleased to see a cat,' she said to the purring creature in front of her. She gently ruffled the fur on its head before standing up. Other than being spooked by a cat – which rolled luxuriously onto its back, begging for more attention – Alice didn't get a ghostly vibe in the kitchen at all, much to her relief. She turned the light off and closed the door behind her as she left, and made her way up the hall into the next room.

The door slowly creaked open as she pushed it. The room was completely dark, aside from a small light towards the far end of the room, a red glow shining through the dark. Feeling around for a light switch, Alice struggled to reach behind the bookcase which was positioned immediately next to the door. She couldn't find the switch. Reaching for her phone, she turned on the torch and shone the light ahead of her and into the room.

It was a fairly narrow room, but seemed to run the full length of the house, and the walls were lined entirely with bookcases, adorned with books, ornaments and unopened boxes. At the far end of the room was a large desk, facing out of the window and onto Cadmus Square. A wide-screen monitor sat towards one of the back corners of the desk, its red stand-by light blinking. There was a subtle musty smell about the room, but other than that there was nothing immediately noticeable. As she moved through the room, Alice idly glanced at the bookcases. The place was more cluttered than the rest of what Alice had seen of the house, and she assumed it was being used as extra storage until the Turners had settled in properly.

The light from her phone cast weird and elongated shadows across the room, as jagged and unearthly shapes stretched out and across the walls. Through the corner of her eye, Alice thought she saw something moving in the shadows, but the second she turned to face it there was nothing there and the shadows shrank back away from the torch light. Something seemed to dart by the desk at the other end of the room, and she shone her torch on it. Again, there was nothing there, only the patient blinking light of the computer screen and some very official looking clutter. Then she noticed something. A drawer in the desk, left slightly open. She felt inexplicably compelled to look inside, and against her better judgement to not go snooping through other people's stuff, she approached the desk.

Cautiously, Alice pulled the drawer out, shining her torch into it. Inside, she found a mess of stationery. Jumbled up paper-clips were irrevocably bound together by the mysterious forces which seem to uniquely afflict paper-clips. Scrunched up pieces of paper rustled noisily, and pens rolled about from the front to the back of the drawer and back again. However, something amongst all of this caught her eye. Underneath the clutter was a folder, and she reached in to retrieve it. Placing the folder on the desk, Alice removed the documents and shone her light on it. It was a document, several pages long, and the first page bore the heading "Property Deed Contract." Alice read on.

Lloyd Turner ("Buyer") and Robert Haversham ("Seller") hereby agree as follows:
Property: This agreement concerns the following real property, commonly known as:
32 Cadmus Square, Knightsbridge, London SW7 1DY

She skipped through the rest of the contract, skimming over the terms and conditions as most people are wont to do, looking for something less boring and, ideally, more relevant, such as any encumbrances mentioning that the house was built on top of a burial site, or a requirement to leave the loft untouched lest it unsettle the spirit beings which dwell within. To her disappointment, she found nothing of the sort. However, she did find something which she thought seemed to stand out. Towards the end of the document, just before the signature boxes, was a single clause.

The sale of this property has been conducted in accordance with the will of the late Louise Haversham, former occupant and home-owner. Outstanding mortgage payments and tax accountability are hereby the responsibility of Robert Haversham, son of the deceased.

She heard the stairs creaking as if someone was

coming down, and she quickly put the paper back in the folder, hurriedly stashing it away in the drawer. *I better show Sam this,* she thought, and turned to leave the room. She immediately halted, and stood completely still as she felt her heart leap up into her throat, dive back into her chest, and promptly stop. Standing in front of her was a woman. At first glance, she seemed to be in her sixties and didn't look quite like what one would describe as "real." She stood huddled in an old-looking cardigan, her skin was eerily pale, and her eyes were sunken and tired-looking. She was also almost entirely transparent. Alice reached out with a nervous hand.

'Hello?' She said uncertainly, as her hand slowly made its way closer to the apparition. She could feel her hand shaking. Just as she was about to touch the almost-woman, the figure faded away, completely vanishing from Alice's sight. 'No, no, no... Come back?' Alice said to nothing in particular, hoping the apparition would return. It did not. *Now THIS is something I must tell Sam!*

Upstairs, Sam had been investigating a couple of the rooms. He hadn't set foot in either Charlie's or the Turners' bedrooms, he didn't want to disturb them too much while he was looking around. From what Sam had overheard while upstairs, damp had damaged some of the boxes in the master bedroom, and he could hear the sound of someone vigorously washing down a wall coming from behind the closed door. He thought it best not to intrude, and instead turned his attention to the unoccupied rooms.

The spare bedroom had proven to be an uneventful search, revealing nothing more than the fact that the Turners had hidden most of their unpacked boxes and general clutter in there. The bathroom was the only place left for him to look in to, so he made his way towards the end of the landing.

Pulling on the light cord just inside of the door, the bathroom light flickered into life. It hummed a persistent and irritating hum. He peered around the room in curiosity. It was sparsely decorated, all of the cosmetics and amenities stored away in the numerous cupboards around the room. Above the sink was a large mirror, and next to it a smaller mirror on the front of a cabinet, which appeared to have been freshly cleaned. Sam held up one of the printed sheets of paper in front of it. *This would be the same mirror, then,* he thought as he looked at the words "darkness is coming" written in the steamed-up mirror in the photograph.

Sam waved his wand-like probe around the room, pointing it towards the cabinet and the mirror in particular. It glowed a strange shade of purple, flickering and pulsating unusually. He whacked it against the palm of his hand, and it glowed steadily before fading into inactivity. It started flickering again a few moments later. *Bloody thing...*

It was then that something caught Sam's eye. There was a weird shape forming in the mirror, as wisps and patterns danced in the reflection, coming together to form... Something. It was something vaguely humanoid in form, slowly coalescing and taking shape behind Sam as he stared at it in the reflection. He turned to look behind him, but there was nothing there. Yet the image in the mirror remained. It wasn't quite like a normal human shape, it looked more like a three dimensional shadow, face-less and only partially visible. Its form seemed to shift slightly, and it appeared to be writhing on the surface. As Sam stared at it in fascination, the shadow-person leaned forward and from its faceless head a large, menacing mouth opened wide, revealing sharp, shadowy teeth. It looked like it was screaming at him, but no scream came. Only a long, echoing, hissing noise.

Almost as suddenly as it had appeared, the shadow-person disappeared, its form dispersing into a number of smoke-like tendrils before spiralling away into nothingness.

'Fascinating', Sam muttered, and he quickly checked the probe. Its crystalline tip flickered as it had done before. *Maybe it hasn't been malfunctioning... I best tell Alice.*

As Sam was running down the stairs, he saw Alice emerge from one of the rooms and start running up the stairs towards him. Meeting in the middle of the staircase, they grabbed each other by the arms.

'I've just seen the ghost!' They both announced in unison.

'What, really?' Sam asked, looking a little stunned.

'Yeah, she appeared to me just now in the Turners' office.'

'It just appeared to me in the bathroom mirror.'

'Is that normal? Can a ghost be in two places at once?' Alice asked.

'I don't know. Then again, nothing's normal in th- Wait, *she*?'

'Yeah, and I think I know who she is, too. I'll show you,' she said, leading him back down the stairs.

'Mine was shapeless and shadowy...' Sam muttered.

Back in the Turners' office space, Alice made her way towards the end of the room, where the folder was sat open on the desk, ready and waiting for her. *Didn't I put it back in the drawer?* She was relatively sure she had, although documents aren't really known for moving about of their own accord.

'Here we go. Have a look-see,' she said, handing Sam the contract, and his eyes quickly scanned over the document. 'Could Louise Haversham still... You know, still *be* here?' Alice asked as she watched Sam reading over the contract.

'Not a bad theory. I wouldn't say it's conclusive, but it's something,' he said, putting the contract back in its folder. He started to head back towards the door. 'Oh, and good find, by the way.'

He shot Alice a sideways smile before disappearing back out into the hallway.

Alice grinned, and quickly followed after him.

The probe started to flicker again. Holding it out in front of him, Sam started to slowly spin, tracing a circle around himself with the wand, using it like a compass. The purplish glow began to grow in intensity, it shone brightly for a second before flickering and dimming again, fading to nothingness. Sam pivoted on his heel, spinning back the way he'd came, until the glow intensified again. Fixing the probe on the door ahead, its crystalline tip glowed and flickered erratically. He gestured towards the door and strode across the hallway, pushing the door open and flicking the lights on as he walked in.

'Are you there, Louise?' He asked, raising his voice as he addressed the air, slowly pacing around the large dining table at the heart of the room. Alice watched him from the doorway with baited breath. Nothing happened. 'I call upon the spirit of the house, and I summon thee. Louise Haversham, I know you can hear me. Give me a sign that you're there,' he continued.

'How do you know she's going to be here?' Alice asked. 'How do you even know it's her we're dealing with, for that matter? You just said it wasn't conclusive.'

'I don't, and it isn't,' Sam said, 'but it's all we've got at the moment.' The crystal at the tip of the probe glowed and pulsated. 'Something's here. Just keep an eye out.'

'What are we looking for?'

'Something. Anything. I don't know yet,' he said as he continued to pace around the room.

Sam held the probe up high above his head as he marched around the perimeter of the room. The crystal continued to pulsate, stronger and faster than before, and it started to emit a high-pitched noise which made Alice's ears twinge. She thought she could hear something else, like a distant voice calling from somewhere else, but she couldn't hear what it was saying. She suddenly felt the sensation she'd experienced in the living room. Pressure began to rise in the room, and her ears started to feel muffled, as if she was underwater. Just out of the corner of her eye, Alice thought she saw something move, and without a moment's hesitation she shouted.

'Duck!'

With that, one of the chairs took flight and launched itself towards Sam. He immediately crouched and felt the chair soar over his head. It hit the wall just behind him, snapping off one of the legs. The probe carried on emitting its high-pitched whine. A cabinet filled with china began to shudder, and the crockery rattled uneasily. Sam stood up again and pointed the probe directly at it.

'Louise! If that's you, I command you stop this.' His words apparently fell on metaphysical deaf ears, as the cabinet doors flung themselves open and launched an expensive looking teacup in his direction, followed by a projectile fork and a spinning plate. He narrowly dodged the airborne crockery, and avoided being stabbed by the flying fork, hitting the floor and crawling beneath the table for cover.

'Stop that thing from making that noise!' Alice shouted at him as a series of knives hurled themselves in Sam's direction, embedding themselves in the tabletop. She'd retreated back to hide behind the door, using it to shield herself from any more wayward cutlery.

Sam hit the probe in frustration with the palm of his hand as it continued to screech its piercing screech. Suddenly, it fell silent. Crockery ceased to take flight, and cutlery stopped throwing itself at him. Things felt a lot calmer, and Alice could sense the pressure leaving the room. Slowly crawling out from beneath the table, Sam cautiously looked around the dining room. Fragments of broken china littered the floor, and cutlery marred the surface of the table like a dart board. He breathed a long sigh of relief.

'What the *hell* happened in here?!' An angry voice bellowed, shaking the entire room. A solitary teacup fell pathetically from the cabinet, smashing on the floor. Sam nervously looked up and into the furious face of Lloyd Turner. His ginger beard seemed to be a deeper shade of red than before, and Sam entertained the idea that perhaps his facial hair changed colour to match his mood. He stood up and dusted himself off, and Alice slowly backed away from the doorway.

'Ghost happened. It's fine, it's gone now. Sorry about the china,' he said, nervously trying to lighten the mood and hopefully diffuse the situation. Lloyd did not seem amused.

'Listen, I allowed you into my home simply to humour my wife's superstitions. I don't believe in ghosts, and I certainly don't believe you're a detective of any variety,' Lloyd spoke with a sinisterly calm and collected voice. He was no longer shouting, but he still spat his words out with just as much anger. 'I was willing to tolerate you for so long, but when I come down here to find you trashing *my house* just to reinforce your nonsense ghost stories...' He paused, and breathed a furious and exasperated sigh. 'You're no longer welcome here.'

'Mister Turner, I can understand your frustration, but this thing is real whether you believe it or not,' Sam said, making his way over to the terrifying man in the comfortable looking jumper. 'I am so close to having this whole situation sorted. Just give me another hour, and I promise we'll be out of your hair.'

'Let him finish his work, dear,' said the voice of Elena, who now came and stood by the side of her still fuming husband.

'But j-just look at this place!' Lloyd exclaimed, waving his hands wildly, gesturing to the state of the room.

'I know, I know... Just give Sam another hour, and if nothing's changed by then he'll have to leave.'

Lloyd's face visibly contorted into an image of pained irritation before spitting through gritted teeth, 'fine.'

'An hour is all I'll need, and I'll be gone' Sam said, 'and I promise I won't break any more of your stuff. Now, if you'll please join me in the living room, I'll let you know what I think is going on here.'

Sam, Alice and Elena took their seats by the fireplace in the living room. The fire had now died down to just a few crackling embers. Lloyd stayed standing in the doorway, staring at the floor in disbelief, his dumb-founded gaze fixed upon Sam's chalk pentagram.

'You've drawn on my carpet,' he said in a voice that was so devoid of emotion it was marginally more terrifying than when he was shouting.

'Necessary to ward off negative energy and malicious spirits. If I'd drawn these symbols in the dining room, you'd still have a complete set of china,' Sam said. Lloyd just glared back at him.

'Anyway,' Sam started to explain, 'a poltergeist that breaks kitchenware, plays with the lights and leaves foreboding messages on mirrors, suddenly ups its game and starts throwing books at people and causing serious damage in the dining room. This started out as a fairly benign haunting, but it seems our arrival has agitated things.'

'From the moment we walked through your door, she knew why we were here, and she's trying to scare us off,' Alice prompted.

'So far, so obvious... But poltergeists don't tend to change their behaviour just because of who they're haunting. Some are malicious and go out of their way to cause harm, and others are just the nuisance pranksters of the spirit world. This one I thought would be the latter, but she's now on the offensive,' Sam said. He could see the perplexed looks on the Turner' faces. 'My theory is that the spirit that haunts this hous-' He was interrupted mid-sentence as the lights began to flicker again. The four of them looked around the room. Alice readied herself for something to happen.

'Bloody fuses again...' Lloyd mumbled.

The lights went out completely, and an eerie stillness descended on the room. The grandfather clock stopped ticking, and the final embers of the once-lit fire ceased crackling. The room was plunged into darkness. Then nothing happened. No books flew off the shelves, no crockery spontaneously broke itself, and no furniture was up-turned. Sam stood up in nervous anticipation. Alice held her breath. It felt as if time had come to a stand-still. Still nothing happened.

After a few moments had passed, the lights suddenly burst back to life, lighting the room up again, and the grandfather clock resumed ticking. With a relaxed sigh, Sam sat back down.

'It's fine,' he said as he took his seat, 'we're safe as long as we're in this room.' They'd only just settled back down when a terrified scream echoed throughout the house, and the Turners were out of the door in an instant.

Following the sound of the scream, Sam bounded up the stairs with Alice not far behind, and darted into the bedroom of Charlie Turner.

Inside, a calmer looking Lloyd was now stood at the foot of a bed while his wife knelt by the side of it, cradling their son. Sam hovered in the doorway, as the child repeated through terrified sobs, 'they're going to get me.' He looked up from his mother's arms and saw Sam and Alice stood in his doorway. He wasn't too concerned about Alice's presence, but it was an unnerving experience for the little boy to see this tall man he'd never met before, in a coat and hat and clad all in black, standing in his doorway and looking at him with an emotionless stare. Charlie tightened his grip on his mother and cried.

'Make them go away.'

'It's all right, Charlie. They're here to help get rid of your nasty dreams,' Elena said soothingly. Charlie still clung tightly to her. Sam shifted where he stood, looking more than a little awkward.

'Yes,' he said, and looked as if he was going to say something else, but decided not to. Alice gently pushed past him and knelt by the side of the bed also.

'Hey Charlie, I'm Alice.' The little boy stared back at her with big, watery eyes. 'Can you tell me a little about your dreams?' She asked softly. Charlie shook his head, burying his face in his mother's shoulder.

'He's had them almost every night for weeks now,' Elena said, gently stroking her son's hair, 'always around this time, a little after midnight. He dreams he's being chased by monsters-'

'What kind of monsters?' Sam interjected.

'Shadow monsters,' mumbled Charlie.

'It's just a dream, son, they can't get to you. Go back to sleep,' Lloyd said. He still stood at the foot of the bed, looking disconnected from the rest of them. Charlie seemed less than convinced that his dreams couldn't harm him.

Still standing in the doorway, Sam surveyed the room. If Lloyd Turner seemed disconnected from everything else going on, Sam Hain was on a completely different plane of existence. He scanned his eyes over the whole of the room. *Curtains closed, unmoving; no breeze, windows shut; comfortable temperature, double-glazing,* he mentally catalogued what he could observe of the room. *Wardrobe doors closed, mirror covered, night-light on. Muted décor. Nothing present in the local vicinity conducive of usual externally produced nightmares. Conclusion: spooky things.*

'Alice?' He said, gesturing with his head for her to join him in the doorway.

'What is it?' She stood up and made her way over to the door. 'Think you've got something?'

'Maybe. Do you feel anything about this room?' Sam asked, lowering his voice almost to a whisper.

'Not really, why?' She shrugged.

'Just try to focus in on it for a minute. Do you sense anything?'

She closed her eyes and tried to tune in with her surroundings. It was hard for her to go on her first impressions of the room. Anything she felt was immediately superseded by the situation; a crying child, a probably-still-angry Lloyd Turner, and the feeling that they shouldn't be there. She felt deeply uncomfortable with being in this little boy's bedroom, in the house of complete strangers, one of whom had been ready to throw them out only a few moments previously.

'I'm sorry,' she eventually said, opening her eyes again, 'I can't *feel* anything. I guess I just can't get past the feeling that we're intruding.'

'*Intruding*. Yes, good word, that's it...' Sam mused. He turned to leave the room, his overcoat billowing out as he span around. 'Mister and Misses Turner, please join me back in the living room. Bring Charlie with you, I suspect the boy needs a nice mug of hot chocolate.'

'I could do with one, too,' Alice muttered to Sam as they left the room.

Once the Turners had congregated in the living room, Sam closed the door and started pacing around the room. Lloyd and Elena seated themselves in the armchairs, with Charlie balanced on Elena's lap and nursing a mug of steaming hot chocolate. He seemed happier now, although he still regarded Sam with a wary eye.

'Mister and Misses Turner,' Sam announced, once they had made themselves comfortable, 'I don't just suspect that your house is haunted – that much is evident – but I believe you have unwittingly moved into the house of someone who has not yet moved out.' Perplexed looks were exchanged around the room. Lloyd Turner stood up, standing toe to toe with Sam.

'I don't know about you, Mister Hain, but I don't see anyone else here.' Sam had never really noticed Lloyd's height before, but now he was stood mere inches away from him, Lloyd seemed to be towering over him.

'Mister Turner, are you familiar with the late Louise Haversham?' Sam asked, trying to straighten his posture and stand as tall as he could. He still felt short.

'What do you know of the Havershams?' Lloyd asked, an accusing look in his eyes.

'She's listed as the most recent resident, before yourselves, at this address,' Sam said, producing his phone from his pocket and showing him a web page from directory enquiries. He didn't want Lloyd to find out they'd been looking through his desk; that was a sure-fire way to get kicked out, if the dining room fiasco hadn't been enough already.

'Yes. She lived here before we moved in. House was sold after she died. We bought it from her son,' Lloyd replied.

'Would I be correct in the assumption that Louise Haversham left this property to her son in her will?' Sam asked, knowing that it was stated in the contract, and he took a few steps back from Lloyd.

'I believe so.'

'According to this,' Sam said, flicking over the page on his phone, 'this was valid as of the end of September. So Louise Haversham was still living here about three months ago. Are you aware of when she passed?'

'No,' Lloyd replied flatly, 'we saw this place on the market last month, and put an offer in almost instantly.'

'So if this is correct, then Misses Haversham has been gone for between two to three months now. I suspect that once the deed to the property had been signed over to her son, he put the house on the market, and you bought it. My theory is that her spirit wasn't ready to move out when the sale went through – she still isn't – and she's letting you know that you're not welcome in her home.'

'That'd be why I felt like we were intruding,' Alice mused aloud.

'Exactly. Our arrival only signified more of an intrusion to Misses Haversham, and she knows we're here to help you with everything you've been experiencing. She probably fears we're going to force her to move on, so she's trying to get rid of us. Not all souls go quietly into the night.'

Lloyd scoffed, sitting back down and casting a sceptical glare at everyone else. 'What rot! You really think that a dead woman is trying to kick us out because she thinks she still lives here? That's impossible.'

'Well then, I ask you to come up with what you think is a more reasonable conclusion. In my experience, the impossible has a certain integrity to it. No matter how impossible something may be, sometimes it can be so bloody-minded that it makes itself possible. Or, at least, very, very improbable,' Sam said. He felt less intimidated now that Lloyd had sat back down. 'Now, if you'll give me a few moments more, I think I can have this whole ordeal resolved.'

He made his way to the door and opened it. Alice stood up to join him, but just as he was passing through the doorway he turned around and faced her. 'No. Alice, wait here with the Turners. If she sees two of us looking for her, she'll start throwing things again. I'll be back before you know it.'

'Oh. Fine,' Alice said, feeling more than a little dejected. She'd been the one who'd found the documents after all, and she had also seen the ghostly woman who she was sure was the soul of Louise Haversham. Sam probably wouldn't even know the ghost's name if it weren't for her. Regardless, she sat back down in the armchair and watched as Sam disappeared out of the door.

'So... Weather's turned out better than expected tonight, huh?' She said, trying to break the tension that now hung in the room. Elena simply 'hmm'd' in agreement. Lloyd just stared blankly at her. Charlie sipped his hot chocolate.

CHAPTER IV

Tentatively walking up the stairs, Sam made his way to the last known location of the Turners' haunting: Charlie's bedroom. It seemed darker in there than it had before, and the glow of the night-light cast eerie shadows up the walls. Simple objects like a chest of drawers became vast, shadowy monsters. He was surprised he hadn't seen the room this way before. If this was how it always looked when Charlie was going to bed, he could see why the boy suffered from nightmares so frequently.

That, and the ghost that haunted the house, of course.

The floorboards creaked loudly as he set foot in the room, and Sam tried to tread more carefully as he made his way further into the room. A similarly loud noise came creaking from the opposite corner of the room. Slowly, Sam approached the opposite corner, reaching into his pocket for the probe. The crystal at the probe's tip fizzled. Something made him feel uneasy in that room, more on edge than usual, and he peered over his shoulder. There was nothing but the shadows and the glow of the landing light. Just as he was about to peer into the dark corner, there was a sudden, loud bang, and Sam wheeled around to see that the door behind him had closed.

'So, we're playing it like that, are we?' He muttered beneath his breath, returning to the door. He pulled at it, twisting the handle, but to no avail. The door had firmly shut itself, and wasn't willing to let him go. He turned back around to face the rest of the room, and caught a glimpse of something moving in the shadows. The ends of the bed-sheet waved gently as if a breeze had blown through, but Sam could feel no draught. Absolute silence had descended upon the room.

'Louise?' Sam called uncertainly into the darkness. 'Louise Haversham, are you there?' Nothing happened. For quite some time, things continued to not happen, but Sam stood patiently, waiting for a sign that the spirit of Louise Haversham was willing to talk with him. The probe's tip suddenly glowed vibrantly, and Sam looked at it with intrigue. He couldn't remember the last time it had picked up on a presence so strong, and just as he was about to take this as a sign that he'd opened dialogue with the spirit, two pillows were hurled at him.

'Louise, I understand why you're upset,' Sam started, attempting to reason with his invisible assailant. The bedsheets began to writhe like a bag of eels who were particularly angry to be in a bag. 'Let's just remain calm about this, I think we can help you...'

He has it all wrong, a voice seemed to echo in Alice's head. She felt herself freeze momentarily, and she glanced at the Turners. They were behaving as if they hadn't heard anything, and by the looks of it they hadn't seen her react to it in any way. For a brief moment, she thought she must've been hearing things, but then the voice came again. *He doesn't understand.* It wasn't like hearing someone speak, and it wasn't like having a thought. It was something like the two things, and somewhere in between them, yet entirely unlike anything she'd ever experienced. She didn't know what to do. Leaning her head back against the armchair, she closed her eyes and tried to focus on the voice. It didn't speak again.

Who are you? She thought, and in an instant her mind's eye was flooded by images of the property deed contract and the spirit of Louise Haversham. She tried to focus on the apparition she'd seen in the Turners' office, concentrating on engaging the voice in conversation. *Is this Louise?* There was no reply, but Alice felt like she was right. There was another stretch of silence, but eventually the voice came again.

Yes. He has it wrong. Not me. Them.

Them? Who are they? Alice asked in her mind.

Shadows. Darkness. They're coming... The voice uttered.

Darkness is coming? Alice felt an affirmative wave flow through her.

Through the portal. The portal is open.

What portal? Where? What?

I came with a warning to deliver. They're coming. The voice was starting to feel more and more flustered. *THEY'RE COMING.* It seemed to scream inside her mind and, jolted by the force of the scream, Alice lifted her head, her eyes wide open. The Turners stared at her for a second, confused and concerned at the same time.

It was then that Alice noticed something was amiss. Smoke had started filtering into the room in thick, black plumes. It swirled up and around, moving in an almost snake-like fashion, not like smoke at all, and Alice felt a deep sense of uneasiness. It began to spin violently around, circling her and the Turners, and as it came closer she could see that it wasn't smoke. It was like a school of eels. Oily shadows swarming around and around, but at no point did they cross the boundaries marked out by Sam's chalk symbols. Alice had seen something not too dissimilar in her dreams around the time she first met Sam. She looked at the Turners, but they didn't seem concerned in the slightest. It was as if they weren't even aware that plumes of smokey, oily, flying eels from another dimension were swimming around them. The only one who seemed to actually see them was Charlie, who tightly clung to his mother in mute fear while he watched them swirl around the room. Neither Lloyd nor Elena seemed to notice Charlie's concern.

'How much longer do you think it'll be?' Lloyd mumbled, his patience wearing incredibly thin.

'Hopefully not much longer,' Elena replied, 'but I'd rather he did his job properly and not rush it.'

The shadowy entities continued to swirl around the room, completely unnoticed by the Turners.

'I'll, uh... I'll be back in a second. Just going to check on Sam,' Alice said, standing up and moving cautiously towards the door. The Turners nodded in acknowledgement. She looked at the symbols drawn on the floor. The shadows had yet to cross them. Sam was right, it did keep them at bay. Alice withdrew the pendant from around her neck and clutched it tightly to her chest, standing just short of the swirling darkness. She took a deep breath, and plunged herself into the shadows.

The Turners watched with curiosity as Alice took her bracing breath and made a single dramatic step forward, before walking out of the room with slow, wobbly steps. To them, it seemed as if she thought she was jumping off of a diving board. Lloyd shook his head. 'Strange girl.'

The shadows were not quite as thick out in the hallway, and with every step forward she took, Alice could see them parting in front of her. She stopped holding her breath, and knew that for as long as she held on to the pendant they couldn't reach her. Wading through the smoke-like eels which now covered the floor, she made her way towards the staircase. The shadowy beings slithered and writhed, curling around bannisters, crawling up the walls and across the floor. More swooped down through the air as she was making her way up, parting just in front of her and weaving around. She struggled to suppress a shriek, letting out a squealing whimper, but she carried on.

The upstairs was mostly empty of these entities, as if the majority of them had headed downstairs, which made Alice feel much more comfortable. When she reached the door to Charlie's bedroom, it was shut. She turned the handle and pushed, but it seemed to be jammed shut.

'Sam, you in there?' She called, her head pressed against the door.

'Yep,' came the response.

'Can you let me in?'

'Umm... I'm a little indisposed at the moment.'

'For God's sake...' Alice muttered, and she shoved herself against the door. It opened with a sudden and unexpected ease, and she stumbled into the room. She looked around, and for a moment she couldn't see Sam anywhere, but then something drew her eyes upward. On the bedroom ceiling, pinned by a duvet, was a rather disgruntled looking Sam.

'Louise and I had a bit of a disagreement,' he said. 'I said she should just accept that someone else now lived in her house, and she threw me up here.'

'It's not Louise,' Alice stated, taking a few cautious steps into the room.

'Well who've I been talking to then?'

'I don't know, weird oily-shadow eel things! They're everywhere. We need to do something. I think Louise told me they were coming from a portal somewhere.' She looked up at the occult detective being held captive by a gravity-defying duvet, and her mind's eye could see the faint outlines of smoke-like beings pinning him to the ceiling.

'Ooh,' he mused, 'a portal. Of course...'

'Apparently,' Alice nodded. 'Now what do we do? How can I get you back down?'

'They took the transphasic probe,' he exclaimed, wiggling around inside the duvet and eventually producing an arm from within its folds. He pointed down at the floor, and Alice could see the wand-like device. She darted over to it, picking it up and waving it aloft.

'Now what?'

'Point and hum!'

'Point and hum?'

'Point and hum!'

Alice pointed and hummed. She could feel the device gradually starting to hum too, vibrating in harmony with her, and the crystalline tip began to glow brighter and brighter. The device's humming intensified, eventually growing to such a volume that Alice could no longer hear herself over it.

'You can stop humming now, just think about whatever is keeping me up here and force it to release me,' Sam said, and Alice stopped humming. She turned her thoughts to the things that were pinning Sam to the ceiling, focussing on them disappearing. The device carried on humming for a few moments and, with a judder and one final, high-pitched sound, it fell silent. It was as if someone had turned on an extraction fan, as the shadowy forms Alice thought she could see were suddenly dissipated. Almost instantly, Sam fell from the ceiling, enveloped in the duvet and plummeting head-first onto the mattress below. There was a soft thud, and a plume of feathers rose up from the impact. From amidst the feathery cocoon, Sam's head emerged, grinning up at Alice.

'Good work.'

'What on Earth is this... This... Oojamaflip?!' Alice asked, throwing the thing back to Sam. It landed on the bed just in front of him. He grabbed it, getting up off of the bed in the most ungraceful manner.

'What do you think it is?' He asked in response, holding it up in front of her.

'A kind of techno-wand type thingy?' She didn't know, otherwise she wouldn't have asked. As far as she had been concerned, it was just a thing that glowed and made high-pitched noises when there was stuff. Now it was a thing that glowed, made high-pitched noises, hummed and could disperse shadow-eels.

'It's a multi-functional transphasic energy probe. It utilises the crystal's dominant oscillatory rate to detect variances or fluctuations in the Akashic Field. It can also interact with the Field, using Akasha energy to project and enhance the user's magickal will. You hum, it resonates and bonds with your psychic signature and frequency, and interfaces with your thought patterns,' he explained as he dusted the loose feathers off of his coat. He marched purposefully towards the door, paused and turned back to Alice. 'So, yes. Techno-wand.'

The probe glowed steadily as Sam walked out onto the landing, waving it around in front of him like he was trying to fend off a particularly persistent wasp. Clutching the pentacle close to her chest, Alice followed him.

'You do know that the stuff you say makes no sense whatsoever, right?'

'It probably doesn't, but that doesn't stop it from being right.' He continued to wave it around in front of him, and Alice could see the shadows parting ahead of him as they'd done with her and the pentacle pendant.

'So how *do* you know this stuff?!'

'I told you, I had a Guide. Now are we going to spend the rest of the night playing Twenty Questions, or shall we seal off this portal?' Sam stopped in his tracks, and took a few paces backwards. The transphasic probe glowed a peculiar shade of purple and made a disconcerting buzzing noise. He took a few steps forward again, and the buzzing ceased. Stepping back, the buzzing started up again. Pointing it upwards, the buzzing became more high pitched.

'The loft,' Sam said, pointing to the loft hatch at the other end of the landing, 'it's in the loft.' He made his way over to it, and stood directly beneath the hatch. 'Still got the pendant?' He asked, turning to Alice. She nodded. 'Good, hold on to it.'

'It's got me this far, I'm hardly going to let it go,' she said, still clutching on to it. 'You could've used it earlier, why didn't you take it with you?'

'I wanted to make sure it'd keep you safe while I was trying to sort things out... I thought I was talking to a misunderstood spirit, not entities from beyond the void.'

Sam reached up and pushed the hatch. It made a clunking sound, but nothing happened. He pushed again and the door came swinging down, knocking his hat off in the process. He ducked down, grabbing his hat, and looked back up into the darkness of the loft. It was pitch black. Pulling the ladder down with a loud *ker-clunk*, he led the way, climbing up into the blackness beyond, transphasic probe pointing ahead of him at all times.

In the darkness of the loft, Alice fumbled around with her phone to turn the torch on. Light emanated from the phone and illuminated the room directly ahead of them. The loft was surprisingly spacious: the roof was high enough for Sam to stand almost upright, and there was plenty of room to move around. Bags and boxes littered the area, strewn about almost haphazardly, and a mound of black plastic bags were congregated around the base of a limbless mannequin, like offerings to a strange idol.

Standing just within the lip of the hatch's

opening, Sam pointed the transphasic probe around the room. It pulsed and glowed, and Sam slowly followed the direction it guided him in. He beckoned to Alice to shine the torch in his direction, and as the light panned across the room it revealed the other things in the loft: more boxes and bags, pieces of an old bookcase, and then nothing. It wasn't that there was nothing there, but it was quite literally a gaping hole of nothingness. A space entirely devoid of anything. Alice's eyes struggled to make sense of it, and her head began to ache. Try as she might, Alice couldn't even begin to comprehend it. Her torch couldn't shine a light on it, and she couldn't even look at it.

'What am I looking at? Is that the portal?' Alice asked, her voice quavering slightly. She couldn't wrap her head around what was in front of her, and she had to turn away from it.

'You're not looking at anything. It's the Void. The vast expanse of the unknowable which exists beyond reality. Just try not to look at it too much, it could drive you just a little bit mad.' Sam kept his gaze fixed on Alice, trying to keep his eyes from looking directly at it as he stared obliquely. 'We can't even begin to comprehend it, it exists beyond our normal senses, and yet our brains still try to fathom its existence. Or rather, non-existence. Something must've generated a massive amount of energy in the Akasha to rip a hole like this...'

Sam lifted the transphasic probe and pointed it at the Void portal. It glowed a peculiar shade of indigo again, and started to screech irritatingly. Alice looked back to see what was happening, but immediately snapped her head away from it. It was as if the act of simply trying to look at it burned the inside of her mind like the worst of migraines. The screeching techno-wand didn't particularly help matters in the head-ache department either. A weird sound, almost like a muffled rushing wind and running water, burbled from the Void's "surface," and from the corner of her eye Alice could see it shifting and swirling like water down a drain.

'Hold on to the pentacle, and whatever you do, do not let go!' Sam said, and he turned to look directly at the portal. The Void glared back at him, and he squinted to try and focus on it.

'What are you doing?'

'I'm fixing it. Just hold on to the pentacle!'

The beings of shadow began to rapidly rise through the floor of the loft, twisting and writhing through the air. They spiralled up and around Alice, brushing past her legs and spinning around her head. She clutched the pentacle pendant tightly and stood her ground, suppressing the urge to run screaming from the loft. The things coiled around Sam, wrapping themselves around him and almost completely concealing him from Alice's sight. As they continued to twist their way around the two of them, she felt a twinge and saw some of them pass through her stomach. She winced at the sensation. Then she felt the pull. It was a sudden tugging, pulling on the pendant and drawing it in towards the Void like the suction of a hoover. The smoke-eel things coiled around the hand Alice was clutching hold of the pendant with, and the pull increased. She held on tightly until her knuckles turned white, refusing to let go of it.

Clouds of the smoke beings were suddenly sucked towards the Void portal, spiralling into the seeming nothingness, swirling around and around as they fell into the event horizon. The entities started to fall off of Sam and Alice, being pulled away from them and into the ever-waiting, gaping maw of Void space, and the pull on Alice seemed to grow stronger. Pressure began to build up in her head, as if she'd been hanging upside down for quite some time, and she was drawn inexorably towards the Void. She could almost see it now, as the smoke beings were dragged into the swirling chaos, but still what lay beyond was impossible to see, and she could feel the unusual coldness of the Void approaching. She could feel herself being pulled in closer and closer, and she looked back. Shadows flew past her head, clouding her vision, but she could see Sam a short distance behind her.

'Do something!' She screamed, but no noise came from her mouth. Her cries fell silently into the Void. The chain around her neck snapped, and she struggled to hold on to it. The pentacle began to slip from her grasp, dangling from the end of its chain and leading her in towards the portal. She dug her feet deeper into the floor, bending her knees to try and stop the inevitable, but to no avail. She was being sucked in and there was nothing she could do about it.

Thank you, a voice echoed in Alice's mind, *thank you for listening.*

Suddenly, Alice was pulled off of her feet, she could feel herself falling straight towards the portal. Everything seemed to come to a stand-still, as if time had come to a stop, and Alice was convinced that this was the last moment she'd ever have. She closed her eyes, and awaited whatever was to come next.

With the slurping noise of the last remaining water going down a drain, the Void portal collapsed. Alice hit the floor with a thud, no longer being drawn in towards the gaping nothingness, and looked up to see the nothingness starting to recede. It fell in on itself, spiralling away and compressing down to a single point the size of a pin-prick, and then nothing. But not the same nothingness as before. It was now just a normal loft space, without any Void portals or smoke-eels. Alice stood up. The pendant fell limply in her hand, succumbing to normal gravity now the Void was no longer sucking her in. She breathed a long sigh of relief, and turned around to face Sam. He was gone, his hat resting on top of the mannequin's head.

'Sam?' She called out uncertainly. 'Sam?'

'Hello,' came the familiar voice, and Sam bounded up from the floor in the same spot the Void portal had been.

'Bloody hell, I thought you'd been sucked in!'

'Thankfully no, but look,' he said, holding up a crystalline object. It was an oval, quartzite stone, the right size to fit in the palm of a hand, and was perfectly formed. Around the circumference of the crystal was a series of intricately carved symbols, and in its core was a weird spiral-like pattern. 'Void crystal,' Sam announced, 'always wanted to see one of these. And you were right, you know.'

Alice looked perplexed. 'About what?'

'Louise. She came to warn the Turners of the portal, but when they wouldn't listen she had to try a more direct tactic.'

'So that was-'

'She helped plug the portal. Now as long as this stone remains inert, it won't be coming back.' Taking out a handkerchief, Sam wrapped up the Void crystal and pocketed it. 'It's in safe hands now,' he said, retrieving his hat from the mannequin and giving it a cursory 'thank-you,' and started heading back down the ladder out of the loft.

'Where's Louise now?' Alice asked. She tried to listen for the voice in her head and tried to feel the presence of the spirit of Louise Haversham. She couldn't feel or hear anything. Sam turned and looked at Alice, an apologetic uncertainty in his eyes.

'I don't know. She's probably returned to the ether now... She used the portal to interact more easily with the world, but now it's closed she probably can't come through so easily,' he said, 'she'll be around, though.'

'Do you know how, or why, that Void crystal

thingy was here?' Alice asked.

'I'm afraid I don't know that either,' Sam said with a resigning sigh. He pulled back the handkerchief slightly to show Alice the crystal. 'Not every day you see one of these things. Weird magick, even by my standards.'

Everywhere was refreshingly clear of smoke-eels and shadow-snakes. The house now looked like a normal house to Alice, with no entities dwelling just outside of her normal perception, and she felt like she could finally breathe properly. The first light of dawn was peering in through the window above the front door, casting bright beams of light on the once dark hallway.

'Wait, hang on, why's it light? What's the time?' Alice looked perplexed.

'I don't know,' Sam said, and he consulted his pocket watch, 'it's about two o'clock.'

Alice checked her phone. It said the time was 01:57.

'It can't be... Look outside! It looks like it should be about eight o'clock!' Alice said. She wasn't wrong, the sun was very rarely up at two o'clock in the morning.

'Temporal displacement?' Sam wondered. 'Maybe the Void portal sucked in localised time, too? What felt like minutes to us could've easily been hours everywhere else...'

'Well that's not at all confusing,' Alice said.

'Anyway, not a word of what went on up there to the Turners. They had a poltergeist problem, and we fixed that problem. They needn't know about the Void or entities or missing time. Just that things are back to normal.'

'Okay,' Alice nodded, and she opened the door.

'Good news, Mister and Misses Turner!' Sam announced, flinging his arms wide open. 'Your problems are solved!'

'About bloody time,' Lloyd grumbled, standing up and immediately making his way out of the living room.

'Thank you, Mister Hain,' Elena said, and she rolled the now-asleep Charlie over, propping him up against the arm of the chair. 'Charlie's certainly calmed down, so whatever it is you've done has worked.'

'Bollocks!' Came a shout from the hallway, and the form of Lloyd Turner shot past the living room door in the direction of the kitchen. 'What's the time?! We must've bloody fallen asleep. I'm going to be late!'

Elena looked confused. 'What on Earth's he on abou-' She stopped mid-sentence as she noticed the daylight flooding into the hallway. She made her way over to the living room window, and pulled open the curtains. Sure enough, a bright winter's morning greeted her. 'I guess we must have nodded off for a while there...'

'Sorry to have kept you all up for so long,' Sam said, 'it took a while, but I don't think you'll be having any more hauntings any time soon.'

'Not a problem, Mister Hain. I appreciate

whatever it is you've done here. Let me brew you both some tea, you're probably more exhausted than us!' She said, and she made her way out to the kitchen. Sam wasn't going to turn down an offer of a cup of tea, even if he had somehow inadvertently caused this family to lose six hours.

Sam and Alice were saying their final goodbyes to the Turners as they prepared to take their leave. Lloyd had disappeared upstairs to hurriedly get ready for work. Elena seemed incredibly grateful, despite the visible tiredness written across her face, and was shaking Sam's hand enthusiastically. Charlie had remained silent for most of the time, drifting off to sleep every now and again with a wobble of the head before waking himself up again. He'd just nodded off again, his head swinging in an arc and back up as he awoke, and he looked up at Alice.

'Morning Charlie,' she said, walking over to him. She wasn't brilliant at working with children, but she felt he deserved to hear something about the night's occurrences too. 'How are you?'

'Tired,' he replied, blinking dazedly at the daylight, 'but okay.'

'Last night,' Alice started, kneeling down beside him, and she paused as she worked out how best to broach the subject. 'Last night, you could *see* them, couldn't you? The, uh, the things. The shadows.'

'They were always in my dreams. The old lady helped me get away from them.'

Alice smiled. 'Yeah, I imagine she did.'

'I wasn't worried,' he added quickly, 'I knew your friend would keep me safe.' Alice looked over at Sam, who had seemingly managed to acquire a croissant without even leaving the room. Flakes of pastry were scattered down his front.

'Yeah... I've not known him long, and I sometimes have my doubts, but he knows what he's doing.'

Charlie looked over at Sam, and tapped Alice's knee. 'No, silly. Your other friend. The man who held the shadows back.'

Alice stared confusedly back at Charlie, not really sure what to say. Her confusion slowly transformed into a look of perplexed wonderment. She remembered being Charlie's age, and how her imaginary friends would deal with the monsters beneath her bed, and helped her escape from her nightmares. The more she thought about it, the more she was starting to question whether they had been imaginary after all. She was about to say something when Sam came over and tapped her on the shoulder.

'Come on, we best be off.' He brushed the croissant flakes from his chest, and Alice looked up at him with a dumb-founded expression. 'It's been a long night for all of us, and I think it's about time we got out of the Turners' hair.'

'Bu-'

'Misses Turner – Elena – it's been a pleasure. If you still feel like this place is haunted in a week or so, give me a call.' He extended a hand, holding out his business card.

'Thank you, Mister Hain,' Elena said, 'and you too Miss Carroll.'

Alice stood back up. 'Yes, a pleasure meeting you, Elena. And tell Lloyd we said "goodbye" too, I don't think he'll be seeing us before we go.'

'I will. He may seem the grumpy sort, but he means well,' she replied, but it sounded more like a poor excuse. 'Take care, and thank you again.'

As they walked down the path and away from the house, Alice turned to take one last look at the place. She couldn't quite explain why, but it felt lighter than when they'd arrived the night before. It could've simply been the fact that she was seeing it in the light of day for the first time, but she knew it was more likely because of what they'd been able to resolve there. Elena and Charlie were stood watching them out of the living room window, waving. She waved back at them, and for the briefest of moments Alice thought she could see the faint shape of Louise Haversham with them. She smiled to herself, and turned to follow Sam.

'Come on,' he said in an unusually cheery voice for a man who'd been awake all night (especially one who'd been closing Void portals), 'let's get some breakfast at one of those cafés. Some of them are probably open by now. They might even have clocks that haven't been temporally dislocated, too!'

The café was significantly emptier than it had

been the night before, but no less warm and comfortable. A rosy-cheeked Alice reclined luxuriously on one of the cushiony sofas, her coat and scarf draped over the back of the seat. She sipped from a large mug of hot chocolate, which was piled high with whipped cream and marshmallows, and a decadent slice of rich chocolate cake sat on the table next to her. She was tired, hadn't slept and had apparently been temporally dislocated by a Void portal, but none of that mattered right now. She finally had the hot chocolate and cake she'd wanted last night, and to her this was the perfect way to end the arduous night.

Sat opposite her, leaning over a small ceramic plate, Sam indelicately munched on another croissant. The flakes scattered out across the table with each bite, landing in his tea, clinging to the wool of his coat, and going anywhere that was not the plate positioned immediately beneath him. He had kept his coat on, despite the warmth of the café, and Alice briefly wondered how he'd cope when spring eventually sprang. He'd at least removed his hat, though, revealing the chaotic mass of hair that was contained beneath it.

As she sat across from the occult detective, Alice realised there was no going back now. There was no longer any room for scepticism; she had stared into the Void and witnessed things she never thought she'd experience. These things which she previously believed only existed in the realms of fantasy were now a part of her reality. She now saw Sam in a different light, too. What had once seemed like the weird ramblings of a strange man were now the words of experience from someone who saw the world in a way like no other. Alice was pleased she'd joined him on this adventure.

'Wha' you thinkin' 'bout?' Sam mumbled through a mouthful of croissant.

'Oh, just stuff,' Alice said with a smile. She'd been thinking about what Charlie had said, not able to shake the thought of imaginary friends maybe not being quite as imaginary as the name would suggest. 'I was thinking,' she started hesitantly, worrying if it might sound stupid. She suddenly realised how many things Sam must say on a daily basis which sound stupid. 'The Turners' son, Charlie... He said he knew my friend would keep him safe.'

'Well, I'm glad to have been of service!' He replied, taking a large mouthful of tea which puffed his cheeks out, and gulped loudly.

'He didn't mean you. He meant someone else... Charlie said that there was a man who held back the shadows. Kind of like I dreamed my imaginary friends did when I was growing up. Does that sound mad? It just seemed a bit, y'know...?' Her sentence trailed off.

'Not mad in the slightest. I believe I said to you when we first met that imaginary friends are probably spirit guides. Children are more open to such things, they don't worry about whether or not it makes any sense in the "real" world.' Sam made air quotations as he said this. 'After all, magick is an art of the mind and soul. What people might dismiss as an over-active imagination is likely a world they've simply forgotten about in their day-to-day lives. Not all, but most. Just because you're no longer a little girl who dreamed of friends no one else could see doesn't mean they're not still there, in a sense,' he said. 'I can see you're starting to remember, though.'

In that moment, for reasons she couldn't explain, Alice thought Sam seemed impossibly old. His face was still that of a man in his late twenties, but his eyes looked like those of a wise, millennia-old soul. Despite the strange eccentricities Sam Hain often exhibited, Alice could feel that at his core there was a man far wiser than he'd ever like to let on.

She smiled and nodded with a contented 'hm,' and took a sizeable mouthful of chocolate cake.

When she finally got back home, Alice threw herself onto the sofa and closed her eyes. She hadn't realised quite how tired she was until she was back in the comfort of home. She was just floating off to sleep when a sudden bang startled her awake.

'Ah, look who's home! Where were you all last night? You look exhausted,' Rachel said. She put the kettle on and started to make the pair of them some coffee. Alice simply lay back down on the sofa, closed her eyes and softly laughed.

'I don't even know where to begin...'

ABOUT THE AUTHOR

Bron James is an author of science fiction, fantasy and magical realism. He was born with a silver pen in his mouth and has been making up stories for as long as he can remember. His professional début work of fiction, the first instalment of the *Sam Hain* series of novellas, was first published in 2013.

Born and raised in the south of England, Bron presently lives in London where he writes stories, drinks tea, and dreams improbable dreams.

~

www.bronjames.co.uk

MORE TITLES IN THE *SAM HAIN* SERIES

Volume I
All Hallows' Eve
A Night in Knightsbridge
The Grimditch Butcher
The Regents
The Eye of the Oracle
Convergence

~

www.samhainscasebook.co.uk

Printed in Great Britain
by Amazon